PAL

First published in 2005
by Simply Read Books
www.simplyreadbooks.com

www.windyandfriends.com

Characters, set design, art direction, and diaramas
by Robin Mitchell & Judith Steedman

Photographed by Mia Cunningham for Picnic
Colour separations by Scanlab
Map and endpage drawings by Robin Mitchell

©2005 Robin Mitchell & Judith Steedman
Printed and bound in Italy by Grafiche AZ, Verona

Cataloguing in Publication Data
Mitchell, Robin 1975-.
   Snowy & Chinook/Robin Mitchell, Judith Steedman
ISBN 0-9688768-9-7

I. Steedman, Judith. II. Title.
PS8576.I8865S96 2003   jC813'.6   C2002-911364-4
PZ7.M6949Su 2003

WE WOULD ESPECIALLY LIKE TO THANK

Brady Cranfield for producing the "Snowy" CD

Everyone who performed on the "Snowy" CD
(Please see CD for individual song credits)

Gillian Hunt, Leilah Nadir and Patrik Andersson
for editing assistance

THIS BOOK IS DEDICATED WITH MUCH LOVE TO

Mary & Stella

SIMPLY READ BOOKS

Snowy & Chinook

Robin Mitchell & Judith Steedman

This book belongs to _____

On a frosty winter morning, Snowy and her big sister Chinook sprung out of bed.

They raced to the window and peeked outside.

The sky was blue and the sun was out.

Snow everywhere!

It was Tulip the buffalo's birthday.

The perfect day for a party.

"We must find a present!" whispered Chinook.

"Let's see what we can find."

So off they went.

Shhhh!
It's a surprise.

"Is a snowball the perfect present for a buffalo?" asked Snowy.

"No, too melty," said Chinook. "Let's ask our neighbours for ideas."

"A stick is a useful gift," advised a great grey owl.

"No, too pokey."

"A big rock is nice," suggested the rabbits.

"No, too heavy."

"How about a toothbrush?" muttered a beaver, through a mouthful of wood chips.

"No, a toothbrush is too expensive."

"Snowy, it's getting late," worried Chinook, "we must be getting home."

Suddenly, a warm wind blew across the plains.

It whistled through the woods and tickled the nose of a sleeping bear.

"Is it Spring?" wondered the dozy bear.

"Look!"

The warm, westerly wind had also woken some flowers.

"Tulip loves flowers." cheered Snowy.

"We have found the perfect present," hoorayed Chinook. "Now, let's hurry home for the party."

"Hooray, Hooray!"

On the way home, a fox peeped out at them.

"Did you find a present for your friend?" he quizzed.

They showed the flowers to the inquisitive fox.

He was very impressed.

The excited pair made plans for their party all the way home.

home

a stick?

"Happy Birthday, Tulip!"

"Flowers!"

"Oh, thank you for the lovely gift," cried Tulip.

Then Snowy and Chinook
and Windy and Sunny
and Tulip all tucked into
pancakes and hot chocolate.
until at last they felt sleepy.

It was time for bed.

"Goodnight, Winter."

Goodnight, Snowy.
Goodnight, Chinook.

What is a chinook?

Sometimes, in the middle of Winter, when
it is cold and snow is everywhere, a warm
westerly wind whistles down the eastern
slope of the mountains, and gently warms
the plains. It's a chinook! Just as quickly,
Winter returns, and the snow falls again.
Good-bye chinook.

AUG 1 0 2011